FREDERICK FINCH LOUDMOUTH

by Tess Weaver • Illustrated by Debbie Tilley

Clarion Books

New York

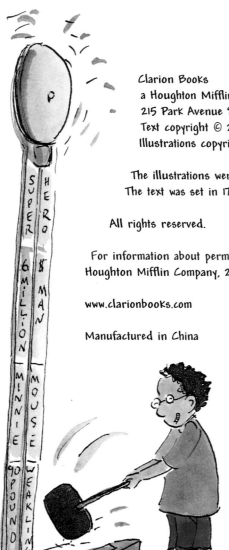

Clarion Books
a Houghton Mifflin Company imprint
215 Park Avenue South, New York, NY 10003
Text copyright © 2008 by Thérèse W. Gullickson
Illustrations copyright © 2008 by Debbie Tilley

The illustrations were executed in pen and ink on watercolor paper, with watercolor dyes.
The text was set in 17-point Andy Bold.

www.clarionbooks.com

Manufactured in China

Library of Congress Cataloging-in-Publication Data
Weaver, Tess.
Frederick Finch, loudmouth / by Tess Weaver.
p. cm.
Summary: After trying and trying to win a ribbon at the state fair,
Frederick finally is rewarded for his true talent.
ISBN 0-618-45239-7
[1. Contests—Fiction. 2. Fairs—Fiction. 3. Individuality—Fiction.] I. Title.
PZ7.W3622Fr 2008
[E]—dc22   2007019114

ISBN-13: 978-0-618-45239-2
ISBN-10: 0-618-45239-7

WKT 10 9 8 7 6 5 4 3 2 1

For Brian, who discovered his talent
—T.W.

For Rosie, with love
—D.T.

Frederick Finch loved the State Fair.
He loved riding the Spunky Spider and Typhoon Mountain.
He loved slurping root-beer snow cones and dipping corndogs in spicy mustard.

Most of all, Frederick loved contests. All the contests.
Even though he never won a prize.

When he was four years old, Frederick leaned back in his boots and

clu-clu-clu-clu-CLUUUUCKed!

at the turkey-calling contest.
But Frederick's shrill voice scared all the turkeys away.

When he was five years old, Frederick entered the checkers contest.
The rules said: **QUIET PLEASE.**
But Frederick couldn't read yet, and he couldn't be quiet.
He laughed and chattered and annoyed everyone . . .
. . . especially the judge.

When he was six years old, Frederick sang in the country music contest.
"A-Hoo-A-Hoo-A-HoooeeEEEE!" Frederick twanged, loud and off-key.
The audience covered their ears. Frederick was pulled offstage.

"Shoot!" said Frederick, clomping away. "Lost again."

On the ride home, Frederick's sister, Elvira, offered Frederick one of her ribbons.
"I've got two first prizes, one third prize, and lots more," she said.
"You can have my pickle ribbon," offered his mother.
"No, no," said his father. "He can wear my barbecue crown. I've got more at home."

"No, thanks," croaked Frederick. "I'm going to win my own prize next year."

"That's the spirit," said his mother.

"Yep," said Frederick. "I just need some practice."

That winter, Frederick worked hard to discover a blue-ribbon talent for the State Fair.

He practiced **duck calling** . . .

singing like a **rock** star . . . .

Some nights, Frederick was so tuckered out from all his efforts, he fell asleep just climbing into bed.

Even so, he tested new talents with high hopes every day.

One spring morning, the list of State Fair competitions arrived in the mail.
Frederick still hadn't discovered his talent.
He didn't know which contest to choose.
"I'm no good at singing," complained Frederick. "**Heck**, I can't even whistle.
I'm loud, but I stink."

"Why don't you try something different this year?" suggested his mother. "Sewing is fun."
"Sewing?" repeated Frederick. "Boys don't sew."
"Sure they do," she said. "Look here."
She pointed to the words BOYS' FASHION FAIR and read aloud: "Shirts, Jeans, Sport Jackets, Safari Jackets."

Frederick couldn't imagine sewing.

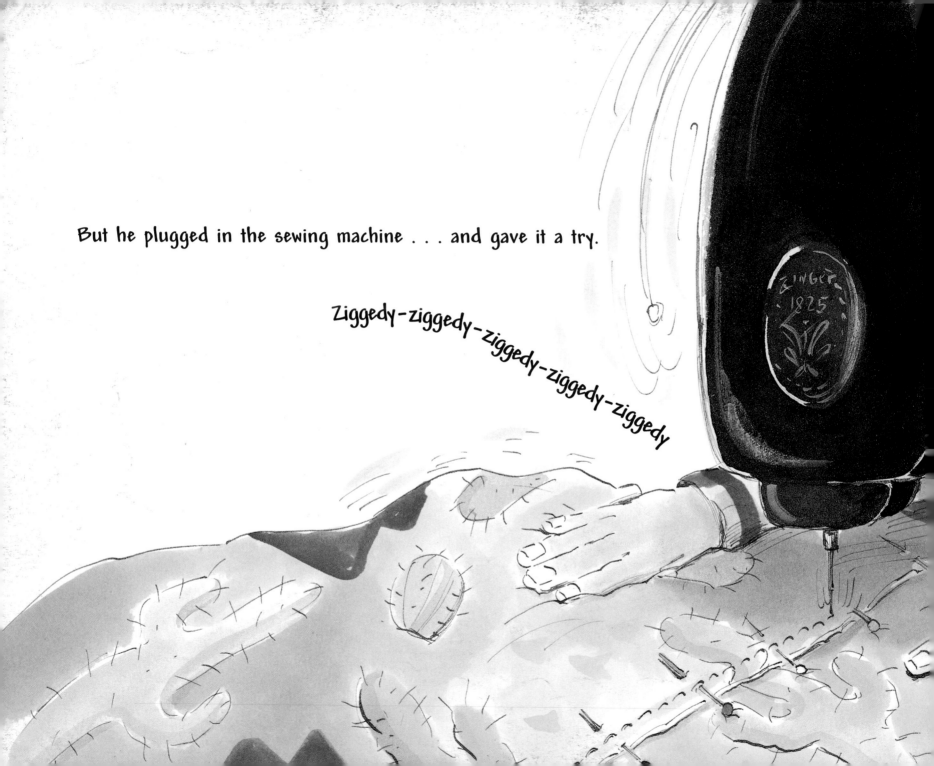

But he plugged in the sewing machine . . . and gave it a try.

Ziggedy-ziggedy-ziggedy-ziggedy-ziggedy

That summer when the Finch family arrived at the fair,
Mrs. Finch unloaded her plumpest pickles.
Mr. Finch brought his lucky barbecue grill.
Elvira yanked her hair for the longest ponytail contest.
And Frederick lit out for the Boys' Fashion Fair.

He grabbed a hanger and pinned a contest number proudly on his shirt.
When he looked around, his heart sank down to his shoelaces.
Hanging next to the other clothes, Frederick's shirt looked bright and peculiar.
Frederick's checks zigzagged into stripes. His polka dots tumbled into tie-dye pockets.
His buttons were outlandish.

"Gosh," groaned Frederick, looking at the plain, perfect shirts next to his.
"Can't I do *anything* right?"
He didn't stay to watch the judging. Instead, he wandered off to find his family.

Along the way, Frederick kicked up dust and pebbles on the path.
He had never felt so low-down discouraged.

When a piece of paper stuck to his shoe, Frederick pulled it off and
saw these words:

NEW CONTEST. TODAY ONLY!
BE THE FIRST TO ENTER.

Frederick tilted his head and kept reading.
"Land sakes!" he exclaimed. His heart did a somersault
in his chest.

Frederick's smile was wider than an ear of corn.

At precisely 10:17 that morning, a booming sound vibrated across the fairgrounds.

It rattled the Ferris wheel, confused the chickens, and tipped over the milking cows.

People looked overhead, expecting to see a cyclone or a rocket ship.

Then they realized it was a human voice they were hearing.

"MOOOOOOoooooooMMMMM!" yelled the voice, "CANNN YOUUUU HEARRR MEEEE?"

Mothers all over the fairgrounds came running.

They left the flower show and the cowgirl-fashion stage.

They scampered out of the butter-carving competition and the tallest-cornstalk contest.

Mothers and grandmothers, great-grandmothers and great-great-grandmothers, followed that loud, insistent voice.

There, on center stage, with his chin tipped up to a cloudless sky, Frederick Finch was a-hooting and a-hollering—"MoooooOOOOmmmmmm! MooooooOOOOO —at the Mom-Hollering Contest!

He knocked the socks off everyone in the audience.
A few other things blew away, too.

"I'd know that voice anywhere!" exclaimed Mr. Finch.
"That's my big-mouth brother," bragged Elvira.
"I always knew he'd win a prize," said Mrs. Finch, wiping away a happy tear.

When he was finished, the governor rushed on stage to shake Frederick's hand.
"Frederick," said the governor, "you'd be real handy in an emergency. Can we call on you if our siren wears out?"
"Sure!" squeaked Frederick.
Around Frederick's proud, skinny neck, the judge placed the championship blue ribbon.
"You could blow the haystacks from here to Kentucky!" said the judge.
"But for the rest of the day,

"SSSSSSSSSSSSSSHHHHHHHHHHHHH!"

"I can do that," whispered Frederick.

And he did . . .

. . . until he stopped by the Boys' Fashion Fair.

"YEEEE—HAAAAAAAAAWWWWWW!"